Shamrock Sean
and the Wishing Well

Brian Gogarty

Illustrated by Roxanne Burchartz
of The Cartoon Saloon

THE O'BRIEN PRESS
DUBLIN

For my wife, Eileen, and children Christine,
Nuala and Ryan, because they believe ...

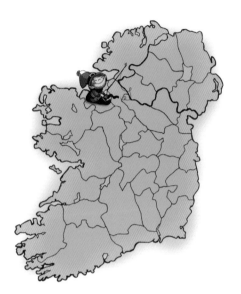

First published 2007 by The O'Brien Press Ltd.
12 Terenure Road East, Rathgar, Dublin 6, Ireland.
Tel: +353 1 4923333; Fax: +353 1 4922777
E-mail: books@obrien.ie
Website: www.obrien.ie

ISBN: 978-0-86278-967-1
British Library Cataloguing-in-Publication Data
Gogarty, Brian
Shamrock Sean and the wishing well
1. Shamrock Sean (Fictitious character) - Pictorial works -Juvenile fiction
2. Wishing wells - Pictorial works - Juvenile fiction 3. Children's stories - Pictorial works
I. Title
823.9'2[J]
1 2 3 4 5 6
07 08 09 10

The O'Brien Press receives assistance from

Editing, typesetting and design: The O'Brien Press Ltd
Printing: Leo Paper Products Ltd

These are the adventures of a lively leprechaun,

He's from the west of Ireland, his name is Shamrock Sean.

He has a little bushy beard, his hair is thick and grey.

He's older than the Blarney Stone if he's a single day.

He loves to eat potatoes – boiled or mashed or roast,

But cabbage mixed with bacon is what he loves the most.

He lives inside a toadstool, beneath a tree of oak,

And if you wander Knock-Na-Shee you might

see his chimney smoke.

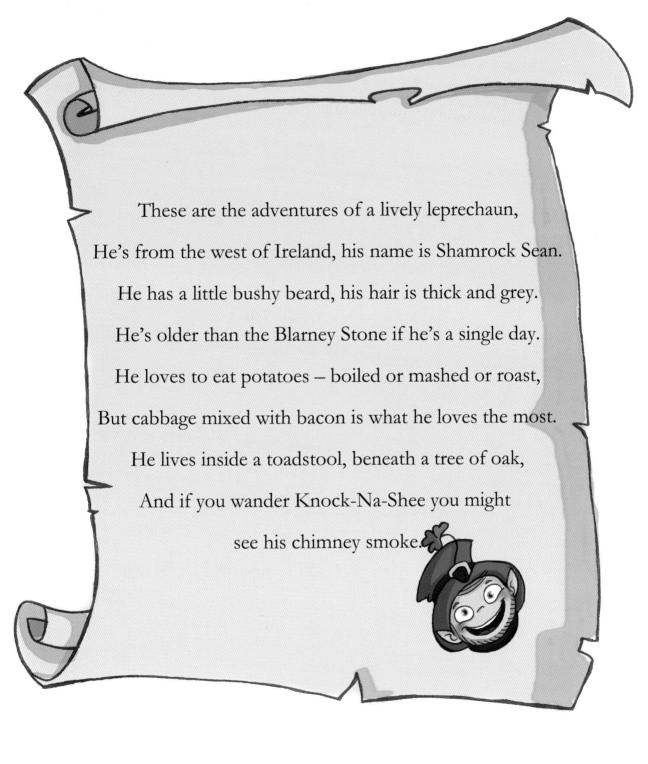

Shamrock Sean got out of bed

And rubbed his sleepy eyes.

He looked out of the window

At the clear blue sunny skies.

'It's such a lovely day,' he said,

I know just what I'll do.

I'll go down to the wishing well

And make a wish … or two.'

He ran across the meadow,

He ran right through the wood,

Until he reached the wishing well

And next to it he stood.

But he couldn't see inside,

For the wishing well was tall.

He said, 'It's not fair!

I'm really far too small.'

He moved a big square stone

And climbed up on the rim.

Then the silly leprechaun

Leaned over and fell in!

He shouted very loudly,

'Oh, someone help me, please!

I'm here inside the wishing well

With water to my knees.'

He got very cold and hungry

In that wishing well so deep.

He tried to climb the wall

But found it was too steep.

He waited and he waited,

It seemed like hours and hours.

Then suddenly he remembered

The wishing well's great powers.

Shamrock Sean closed his eyes

And wished with all his might.

'I wish that I was home,' he said.

– There was a flash of light.

At once he was back home again,

His feet still soaking wet.

'I wished and it came true!' he said,

'It's the best wish I've made yet.'